D0602892

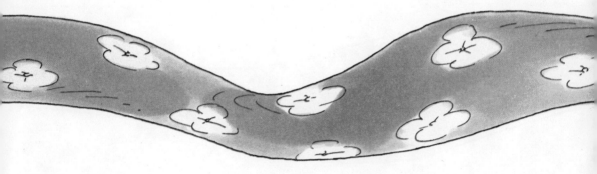

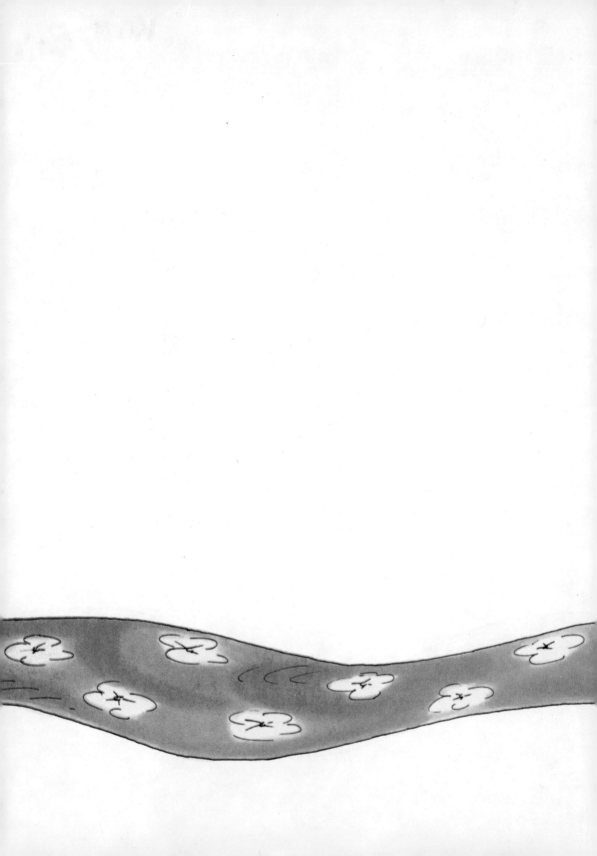

THE
CAT'S PAJAMAS

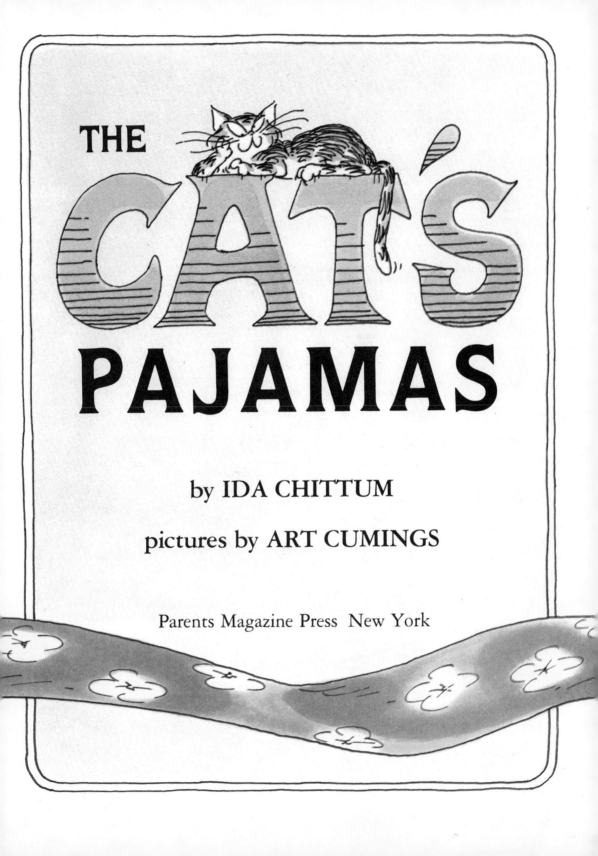

THE CAT'S PAJAMAS

by IDA CHITTUM

pictures by ART CUMINGS

Parents Magazine Press New York

Library of Congress Cataloging in Publication Data
Chittum, Ida. The cat's pajamas.
SUMMARY: Fred spends a lot of time and effort making
his cat a pair of pajamas, but the cat won't wear them.
[1. Cats—Fiction.   2. Clothing and dress—Fiction]
I. Cumings, Art.   II. Title.   PZ7.C4453Cat   [E]   80–10579
ISBN 0–8193–1029–8   ISBN 0–8193–1030–1 lib. bdg.

To eight cats I know:
Arthur, Molly, Max, Liddy,
Nelson, Mouse, Bugs, and Pip...
and to Poo'Chi Kou

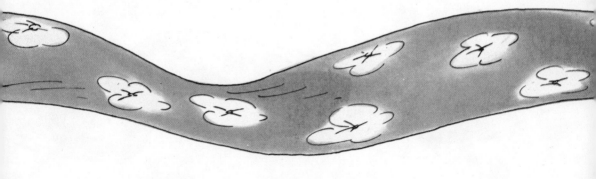

The cat's pajamas
started out as a big
piece of red cloth
with white flowers.

Fred folded the red cloth double
and laid it on the floor.
He placed the cat on the cloth
and drew around her.
He took the scissors
and cut out the cloth
around the crayon line.

Fred held up the two pieces of
red cloth with white flowers.
He said to Red, his dog,
"These are just right for
the cat's pajamas. All I
need is a nice long piece of
red thread to sew them together."

He looked in the sewing box.
He found yellow thread.
He found green thread.
But he couldn't find any red thread.

"Would you like to go with me?"
Fred said to Red.
"I am going over to Mr. May's house
to borrow a piece of red thread."
"Arf, arf!" Red said.

Fred knocked on the door.
Mr. May opened it.
"Hello," Fred said.
He held up the two pieces of cloth.
"These are the cat's pajamas.
All I need is a piece of red thread
to sew them together."

"One second, Fred," Mr. May said.
He went into the next room.
Fred heard Mr. May opening
and closing drawers.
He heard something fall
and hit Mr. May.

Mr. May came out limping.
He said, "Sorry, Fred.
I couldn't find any red thread.
Why not try the family next door."
"Thank you," Fred said.

Fred and Red went next door.
Fred knocked. "Hello," he said.
He held up the two pieces of cloth.
"These are the cat's pajamas.
All I need is a nice long piece
of red thread to sew them together."

The woman at the door shook her head.
She hadn't heard a word Fred said.
Lots of little children behind her
were yelling all at once.
And a baby was kicking its feet and crying.
Fred decided that this was not a good place
to find a piece of red thread.

So he and Red went to the park.
A lady was sitting there with
her poodle and her sewing basket.
"Hello," Fred said.
He held up the two pieces of
red cloth with white flowers.
"These are the cat's pajamas.
All I need is a nice long piece of
red thread to sew them together."

The lady reached into her sewing basket.
She pulled out a nice long piece
of red thread.
"Thank you," Fred said.
He sat right down and sewed up
the cat's pajamas.

Fred and Red started home.
On the way, Fred put down
the cat's pajamas
so he could tie his shoe.

Along came a great big dog
and ran off with the cat's pajamas.
"Stop! Stop!" Fred called.
"You are running away with
the cat's pajamas."

The great big dog leaped over a hedge.
Red leaped over the hedge after him.
Fred ran around the edge of the hedge.

By the time Fred and Red
caught up with the great big dog
running away with the cat's pajamas,
a tall boy had taken them from the dog
and tied them to his kite.

All Fred and Red could do
was stand there
gazing up into the sky,
watching the cat's pajamas
flying higher and higher.

"Doesn't that piece of red cloth with
white flowers look nice as the tail
of my kite?" the tall boy asked Fred.

"Those are the cat's pajamas," Fred said.
"I just made them today."
"Oh," the tall boy said. "I didn't know."

Hand over hand he began bringing down
the kite so he could return the cat's pajamas.
But the kite got caught in the top of a tree.
"Don't worry," the tall boy said.
"I can climb that tree."

So the tall boy climbed the tree,
untied the cat's pajamas,
and tossed them down to Fred—
just as a garbage truck
was passing underneath.
The cat's pajamas fell into the
garbage in the back of the truck.

Fred and Red ran after the truck.
Fred was shouting and pointing.
"What's the matter?"
shouted the driver, slowing down.
"You're driving away with
the cat's pajamas," Fred said.

The driver stopped the truck.
With two fingers he picked
the cat's pajamas out of the garbage
and gave them to Fred.
"Thank you," Fred said.
He held the cat's pajamas far
from his nose as he walked away.

A girl was coming toward Fred and Red.
She made a face at them and said,
"You'd better not get that
dirty old rag near me."

"This is not a dirty old rag," Fred said.
"These are the cat's pajamas.
I am taking them home to wash
and dry them."

When Fred and Red got home,
Fred washed and dried the cat's pajamas.
Then he looked for the cat.
She wasn't in the garage.
She wasn't asleep in the chair next door.
She wasn't on the window sill.

But she WAS curled up fast asleep
in the basket right in the laundry room.
The cat took one look at the pajamas,
hissed, and ran away.

"Now what will I do with cat's pajamas?"
Fred said. He looked at Red.
"Would you like to try on the cat's pajamas?"
"Narf, narf," Red said.
Fred scratched his head.
"I have an idea," he said.

He stuffed the cat's pajamas
with lots of soft cotton,
sewed up the ends,
and put them on the sofa
for a fine new pillow.

That's what happened to the cat's pajamas.
Thank you.

ABOUT THE AUTHOR

Raised in the Ozark Mountains, IDA CHITTUM came
to children's book writing with a background steeped
in the storytelling tradition of that area. When
her own children were grown, she extended the fun
she had telling stories to the written word. Over
the last ten years she has published an equal number
of books. *The Cat's Pajamas,* her eleventh, is her
first for Parents.

Ida Chittum and her husband divide their time
between Southern California and Illinois, where
she still does a lot of storytelling to groups
of various ages.

ABOUT THE ARTIST

Before turning to children's book illustration,
ART CUMINGS worked in films. There he developed
a keen sense of how to make a story move
visually, which he brought with him to his
book projects.
In addition to his illustrations for other
children's publishers, Mr. Cumings is now a
Parents regular, with two other Parents books
to his credit: *Septimus Bean and His Amazing
Machine* (by Janet Quin-Harkin) and *A Good Fish
Dinner* (by Barbara K. Walker).
The Cumings family lives in Douglaston, New York.

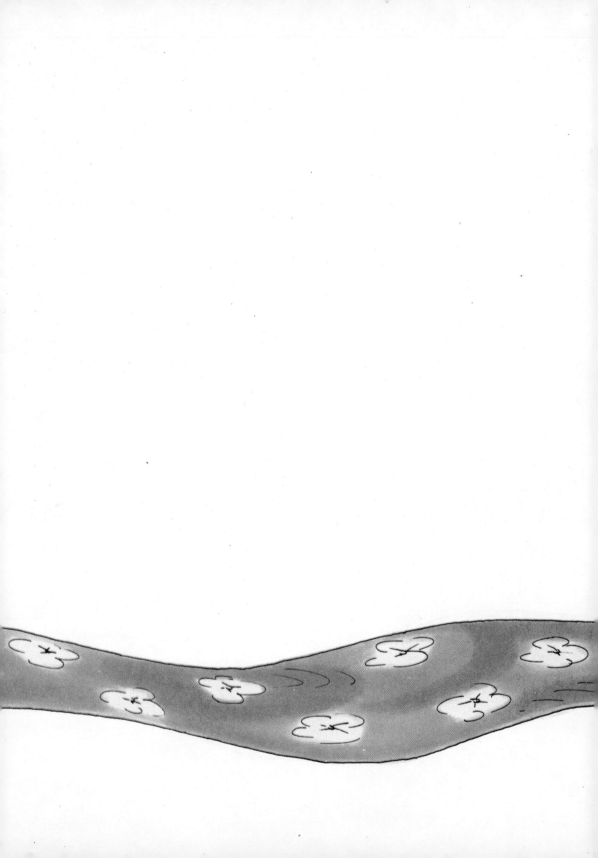

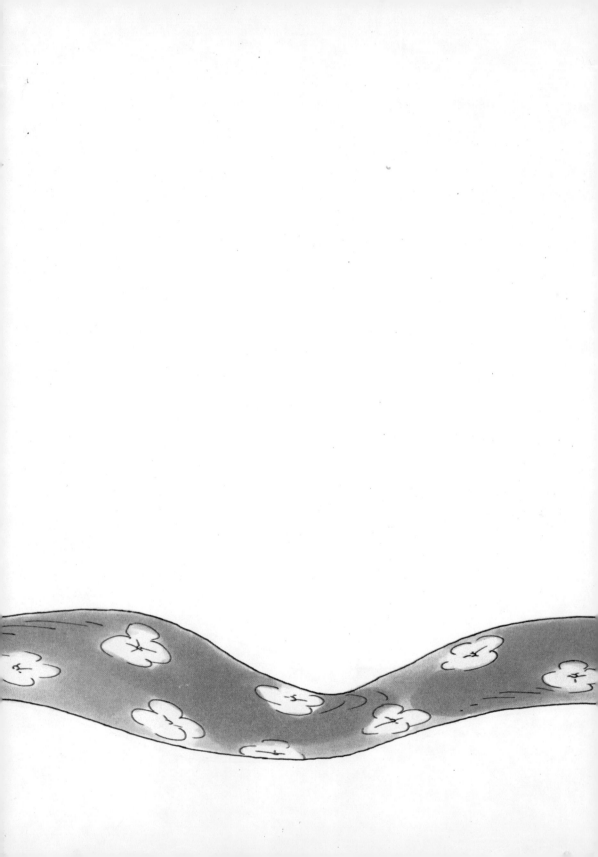